A   Short Story

Collection

By Donna Hernandez

A Short Story Collection

ISBN 978-1-105-44237-7

To my mother for all the encouragement you gave me

ROSES IN THE STONE

His face was scarlet with rage; his nostrils flaring and his breath rapid and forceful as he kicked open the motel room door. He shouted at the girl cowering inside as he waved the gun. "Where are my drugs, you little bitch? What have you done with them?" His bloodshot eyes e seemed about to pop out of his head. Joining him in the room, Tom had never seen his friend so out of control with rage.

She struggled as he dragged her through the hallway and downstairs. There didn't seem to be anyone else around, or maybe they'd spotted the gun and decided to hide. It was that kind of motel.

Tom saw fear in the girl's eyes as she turned towards him. "Tom please tell him. I did not take his drugs.

"I didn't take it. I swear," she whimpered.

"Where are my drugs? Did she take them or not?" He shouted as he twisted around pointing the gun at each one of the men in turn.

Tom's heart pounded in fear as the gun pointed towards him. "I'm telling you. She walked out of here with them. She wouldn't listen when we told her to leave them."

"Where are my drugs?" he demanded one last time.

Tom heard an explosion, then dead silence. Tom watched in horror as, as if in slow motion, the girl jerked backwards and crumbled to the floor with a bullet wound to her head. Blood was pooling under the left side of her head, blood spatter covered the wall. Tom felt something wet on his face; wiping it away he saw gray tissue. Tom could not believe what had happened.

"Oh, my God! What did I do? Okay, okay, she shot herself," the man said forcing the gun into her hand "She got upset and grabbed the gun and shot herself in the head. Okay that is what happened. If we don't all tell the same story we are all going down for murder."

"Shit Tom. We are in big trouble. Someone had to have heard the gunshot," Jack said fearfully.

"Man, we've got to get the body out of here before anyone comes. We'll hide her in the desert and clean up this place fast. If anyone finds her they will think it was done there. Man, I can't go down for murder," Adam shouted. "I have a wife and two kids. I can't go to prison."

Tom removed the gun from the dead girl's hand, pulled a blanket off the bed and wrapped her in it. Adam looked out the door and waved to the other three to follow. He opened the trunk of the car and motioned for Jack to throw the body inside.

They headed out to the desert and found a deserted place far from any dwellings; they laid her in the rocks. Except for the gunshot in the left side of her head and the blood covering her nightgown, she looked like she was sleeping. Reaching down Tom spread her hair over her gown to cover the blood. When he looked in her eyes it seemed as if she were asking him to help her.

As they sped away into the night, Tom knew they could not return to the room, with all the blood and evidence. Who knew if the police were there?

Tom watched from down the street as red and blue lights flashed on the motel. Police were all around searching for something or someone. Just then he saw Sara pull into the parking lot of the motel. Oh my God Sara, Tom thought.

"Sorry miss no one can enter."

"I live here, my room is right there." She pointed to the room police were searching."What happened?"

"This is your room? Where were you tonight?" He asked.

"I was at work. I was there from two until about ten minutes ago. What happened?" Sara tried to look in the room; she saw what looked like a reddish stain on the carpet.

What happened in my room? Is that blood? Oh my God what is going on? Why are they searching my room? Sara thought as she turned back to the officer.

"Miss someone was murdered. The landlord thought it was you. But I see it was not. Who else has access to your room?"

Sara slid to the floor, "Murdered? Who? No one has access that I know. I live here by myself," she stammered.

Sara started shaking as it all hit her. Someone had been killed in her room. She had no idea who or why. This could not be happening, she thought as she was taken to the station.

Meanwhile across town Tom and the other men sat in a room drinking and discussing what they would say if they were caught. Tom shifted uneasily on the bar stool. He was scared out of his mind. What if they arrested Sara? After all it happened in her room.

The body lay in the desert. Detective Todd Roberts shook his head sadly. It never got easier. He turned to Peterson who was first on scene. The rookie was pale and having a hard time keeping his composure. Roberts hoped the officer had it together enough to answer a few questions.

The young girl, who looked no older than twenty, lay with her long brown hair spread out, across her light purple nightgown. To him she looked like a sleeping rose among the stones.

"Detective she was shot close range. She never had a chance. There is no blood so she was not murdered here," Peterson said, then turned and threw up his dinner.

Roberts looked around the scene and saw tire prints a few feet away. All around the body were footprints, from what looked like sneakers. Roberts photographed the tire and foot prints and called in the crime scene unit.

Roberts' cell rang. "Roberts here. Where? The Mansion Motel. Damn. Chief, I'll be right there." He had an intuition his victim was the missing murder victim.

After driving to the station, Roberts entered the room where Sara sat, waiting to be interviewed. Sara looked up, her face wet with tears and confusion.

"Miss you stated no one else had access to your room. If that is true why and how someone did get killed there? Who are you trying to protect?"

Sara looked up at Roberts, her eyes glistening, "I am not protecting anyone. I was at work. I have no idea who was in my room. When I rented the room I was told that no one besides the landlord and me had a key. No, before you ask he couldn't have done it. He's a sweet old man." Sara said shaking her head.

Roberts knew because of her alibi that Sara was not the killer, but there was still the fact that someone else had access to her room and there was no sign of forced entry. They had already found the murder weapon, a Ruger 5 Round 38 Special w/Fixed Sights/Stainless Finish & 2 1/4" Barrel sitting on a small table in the room. The weapon had already been sent to the lab for fingerprints and testing.

The next morning Roberts received a hit on three sets of fingerprints. One set belonged to the victim twenty year old Robin Miller, another set to Adam Wilson age twenty five, and the last set to Tom Jackson age twenty six.

While doing a background check on both suspects Roberts discovered Tom had a history of offenses involving violent crime. Adam had no criminal background that could be found in the database. He had been fingerprinted when he applied to become a foster parent last year.

Heading back to the station, he went to the holding cell where Sara was. Looking at her he did not think that she could be part of this murder. But she had to know something. Where Tom might be. After all he was her brother.

"Sara we found the weapon in your room, and your brother's fingerprints are on the gun. Where is he? When did you last see him?"

Sara's eyes widened at her brother's name. It had been three years since she had last seen or heard from Tom. Now his fingerprints were found on a murder weapon in her room.

"Detective I have no idea where he is, or how his fingerprints were found on a gun in my room, "Sara said looking straight at Roberts. "Are you sure they were his prints?"

"Look the prints belong to Tom. There is no doubt about it. So tell us where he is. Or you will be going down for this murder. Do you want to do time for a murder that he committed."

Sara gasped at his words. Would she really have to do time for a murder? Where was Tom? How was he involved with this? They had been good friends as kids. He would never let anything bad happen to her. Or so she thought.

Tom sat at the bar, nursing a beer. He already knew from TV that they had found the body and he had seen the cops at the motel. It was just a matter of time before they discovered who killed her. He was scared. Tom knew what he had to do. He made a call and waited. He did not want to go down for this and with his past there was a chance he would. After all he never wiped the gun after removing it from her hand. That was enough to incriminate him.

He shifted nervously in his chair, his fingers intertwining repeatedly as he fidgeted. He watched the room, corner to corner, as if he was waiting for something, someone...Tom glanced up as Detective Roberts walked towards him. He recognized his face from the news earlier.

A few hours later at the police station Roberts read Tom his Miranda Rights and began to interview him about the murder.

Tom shook a cigarette out of the crumpled pack as he sat at the table. He was scared. He did not know what happened to Sara or even where she was.

Roberts sat down beside Tom, "Your fingerprints were found on the gun. Tell the truth. Tom tell me about the murder."

Tom took a drag of his cigarette, and told Roberts the whole story. About the stolen drugs, how Adam forced the gun in her hand after the shooting and told everyone to say that she shot herself. "I removed the gun from her hand, after we decided to take her body out into the desert. I did not even think about wiping the prints off. Man I was scared. We were all high but he was like a crazed man. Adam was out of control. He was pissed that she stole his drugs. He took the gun out of its holster pointed it to her and pulled the trigger. He seemed surprised when the gun went off."

Tom told how they went to the desert and laid her out on some rocks. "I knew she was dead, but I can't forget the way she seemed to be asking for help. I will never forget the way she looked."

"Tom we know that you have a history of violent crimes. Why would a man who was never arrested murder someone? What are you trying to hide? Your sister? How is it you were in her room?'

Tom looked up, his eyes filled with tears, "Yes I have had problems in the past. But I'm telling you I didn't kill her. I …. Sara has no idea that I was in her room. I'd picked the lock when she was at work. I needed a place to hang out. Sara has nothing to do with this. I swear. "

Roberts knew that Sara was innocent; he also knew that Tom was a scared man and telling the truth. He had already interviewed Jack and John who told the same story. He didn't want Sara to go to prison anymore than Tom did.

Later that evening Roberts watched as Adam was brought into the station. He was a short stocky man with thinning hair and looked disingenuous. Adam yelled and lunged towards Tom, "You asshole! You were my friend! We all said we would tell the same story! You lied man! You lied!"

Tom turned towards Adam before entering his cell, "I'm not going to prison for you man. I'll go because of the part I played but not for murder."

The End

SILENT MOMENTS

Chris Taylor had been unpopular in high school and now ten years later he was here at his school reunion dressed in a custom-made dark gray suit, pale blue shirt, with a blood red tie. His dull brown eyes hid behind green contacts and his messy black hair was longer.

At school he'd been voted the 'most unlikely to not to succeed' but he proved everyone wrong. Now he was a successful businessperson owning one of the largest and popular photography studios on the west coast. He had made a life that was good and satisfying.

Chris was one of the most sought after photographers; famous models and celebrities graced his studios walls many with him included in the pictures. He frequently dated well-known models. However, no matter what he achieved or accomplished, he had never forgotten his one true love, Rachel.

The night dragged on leaving Chris with the desire to leave early. Chris detested these types of events especially seeing people he had not seen in years trying to impress each other, as if they were something they were not. Chris wasn't the type to talk about his life story or his secret. He patted his coat pocket where he kept his camera.

Chris looked around the room his green eyes widened when he saw her coming through the door with her hand on her husband's shoulder. She looked stunning. Rachel was one of the most popular girls in school, with long brownish red hair, slender long legs and a knockout figure. The tinkle of small bells floated toward him as she laughed at something her husband said. Chris gasped. She was as he remembered. He could not take his eyes from her.

Choking his emotions Chris walked towards her. Maybe I could take one photo to last me a lifetime he thought.

Taking his camera out of his pocket Chris first began taking photos of couples on the dance floor. He roamed the room clicking until there she was standing near the table with a wine glass held in her hand. Her face glowed with a radiant smile as she talked to the others around her. He aimed the camera towards Rachel and focused in. He wanted a full shot of her face so he would have her near him always. The camera shook in his hand as he pressed the button; the flash was bright. The click of the camera sounded loud as he took several photos. She smiled straight into the camera…did she know?

As the night dragged on Chris smiled as he thought of the snapshots in his camera and the girl he had secretively loved for all these years kept in the deepest part of his heart safe from everyone.

As the soft music started, Rachel walked towards Chris. She held out her hand and nodded towards the dance floor.

"Come dance with me." She glanced in the direction of her husband who was drinking at the bar on the other side of the room. Slowly and reverently he took her into his willing arms.

Chris felt the warmth of Rachel's body as they linked arms and glided onto the dance floor. A long strand of hair curled against his hand, as if it had a life of its own. Soft music played in the background and when the lights dimmed, Rachel laid her cheek on Chris' shoulder. Chris wanted this moment to last forever. She felt so right in his arms, if only...

Chris remembered how she felt in his arms the last time they danced. She was so sweet back then just a girl, but now she was a woman. A real woman.

As the last note faded away Rachel looked up at Chris with a shy smile, her blue eyes twinkled. Pulling his head down toward her, she whispered in his ear then turned and walked away.

A few days later Chris sat at the kitchen table and dusted the tarnished gold frame. He unclipped the glass and removed an old yellowed piece of paper with the word Rachel written on it. He placed his favorite photo of her inside, then set it on the mantel and stepped back. Rachel was the most beautiful girl he ever knew, and now she would always be near.

It seemed as if there were many secrets that night, exposed in the silent moments of that one dance. Chris felt an inner warmth and contentment as he reflected back to the last words Rachel whispered in his ear before she left that night. "I have always loved you."

The End

Ninos Del Limbo

My father-in-law Gabriel Hernandez was born and raised in Mexico, he died about 18 years ago at the age of seventy. He was the secretary to one of the presidents of Mexico. When I first met him he told me about a story of children in limbo. I found it hard to believe at first until I really listened to him as he told the story. He was very convinced that all of this really happened. However I was doubtful about the whole thing.

One night roughly midnight he was working in his study typing speeches for the President of Mexico, he suddenly felt his pant legs being pulled at first he thought it was one of his youngest children; he looked under the desk to scold them for being out of bed. There was no one there but he heard the faint sound of a child's laughter.

A couple of nights later as he again sat typing at his desk, the pulling on his pants began again. Suddenly the lamb on the desk turned off with a click and the laughter began again. Ignoring the sound he turned the lamp back on and continued to type. He said that this caused the children to start moving things on the desk, pencils and pens moved from one side of the desk to another. Paper clips were sent flying in the air landed a few feet away. My father in law did not say a word he just continued to type.

Around three that morning he headed to bed. As he lay down he felt his hair, nose and ears being pulled by little hands. He rolled over trying to ignore it, pulling the blankets over his head. However the blankets were pulled off and the pulling his hair, nose and ears started again.

"Leave me alone! Go play with you mother and father!" he shouted as he pulled the covers back over his head.

He heard the sound of laughter and small voices "No, we want to play. We want to play."

This went on for the rest of his life. He would have these children come to play while he was working in the study or while he tried to sleep at night. They continued to want to play with him.

One night he sat some toys up on the table in the living room, He placed each one a certain way, not one toy was touching the other, they were in a straight line. The next morning when we got up the toys were all in a circle touching one another. He asked us if anyone had gotten up and moved the toys. Everyone said no they had not touched them.

That night once again my father in law, sat the toys out on the table this time he place some type of any ink on them that stayed wet and would stain the hands of anyone touching them.

When we got up the next morning the toys were once again moved. My father in law asked to see all our hands, no one had any of the ink on them.

I wondered if my father in law was moving them himself at night or in the early morning before we all go up. My husband said no he would not do that.

I asked him who these small children were and he told me a story that he was told when he was younger. Back in the early 1900's some of the fathers of the church had gotten women with child. They would have the child taken and killed before they were born, and buried under the church. These children were Infants who have died before being baptized. They were in limbo. Not all the children who were in limbo were killed by the fathers of the church some were ones who died when they were born or not to long afterwards. Now I do not know if this is really want happened it is just what I was told.

I then decided to look up Ninos Limbo and I found out that according to the catholic church the "limbo of children" or destination of unbaptized infants has never existed and that is the truth, no matter who despite good intentions and who have been instilled in the people who so childish and unfounded beliefs. Thus, there was no "limbo of the just", which was understood as the place that housed the souls of those who died before the resurrection of Christ."

Now my father in law is not the only person that had been visited by the children of limbo there has been many cases of people in Mexico who have heard and felt them. They are convinced that the children of limbo are real, and they are visited by them each night to play.

Where they are really there or not I cannot say all I can say is my father in law was very convinced that they were and he had them in his house every night up until the day he died. I never heard or felt anything while I have been in the house of my in laws.

So are there really children out there who are in limbo waiting until the day they are set free. Who play all night and move things around, Playing games on the living while they wait for the day they are set free from the limbo they are in.

The End

Sandra's Magical Adventure

"Wake up! Come on, hurry and get up' Sandra shouted as she dashed into her sisters' room. "Today is the big day!"

Lucy opened her eyes halfway, and groaned. "What big day? It is Saturday, and six in the morning."

"Wake me up in two hours" Darlene pulled the covers over her head and went back to sleep.

"It is Medieval Festival today!" Sandra said excitedly. "We'll see knights, princesses, jugglers and there will be lots of food and drinks and my favorite; jousting tournaments. Come on you two we do not want to be late."

"Okay, okay fine." Darlene groaned and pushed the covers off. "Just let me get dressed."

Sandra, Lucy and Darlene strolled up and down the fairgrounds. Sandra' eyes opened wide as she took in all the fun things, a big grin spreading across her face as she watched a puppet show.

Next they went towards the jousting field where two men clad in shining armor sat atop a pair of huge horses. One knight was all in silver, the other had a bright green dragon painted on his shield.

A lady dressed in pink sat high on a platform to the side of the field. She held out a white scarf and released it to slowly drift to the ground.

The two knights took off with their lances pointed straight ahead. Dust clouds trialed behind them as their horses pounded the ground beneath them.

The silver knight hit the ground and rolled to a stop. The green knight raised his lance in victory.

Darlene said something about being hungry and headed towards the pizza shop. Sandra slowly followed behind taking in everything. Suddenly she looked around; both of her sisters were gone. She looked around and saw a door that said "Tavern" on it. Thinking that there is where her sister had gone, she opened the door and stepped through.

Sandra's eyes took a few minutes to adjust to the dimness inside. The large room was filled with people dressed in medieval clothing. A young boy, who looked no older than ten, stepped closer. "Are you here to help find the prince?"

"What? Find the prince? I did not hear anything about that. Is that something new they are including in the Fair this year?"

"Did you not hear the prince was taken by the wizard? Anyone who finds him will be greatly rewarded."

Sandra looked around where was she; the language was a little different than outside. She headed towards the door and looked outside, nothing was the same. The fair was nowhere to be seen, nothing was there,

"Where am I and what is going on?"

The boy looked at Sandra like she was crazy. "You are in the Kingdom of Laster. Prince James has been taken and the king is offering a reward to anyone who rescues him. The wizard took him to his fortress where he will stay unless the king turns over the kingdom to him."

"Don't you have knights that do that sort of thing?'

"Everyone that has tried never returned." The boy said as he waved towards the west.

Sandra set out for the fortress. As she got closer the sky faded to a gray, and then darkened to black. The evil of the wizard's power reached out far and wide.

Sandra traveled most of the day before reaching the massive fortress which loomed before her. Waves of dark clouds hung over the castle, the dark gray stone were covered with moss and thorn bushes. A shiver ran down Sandra back.

As she slowly approached the fortress she was startled by a loud noise. The sky turned even darker and smoke was everywhere. Sandra looked up and saw a three headed, fire breathing dragon swooping down towards her.

Sandra jumped to the side of the fortress wall just as the dragon flew pass. Sandra took a deep breath, in relief.

Sandra crept quietly up to the fortress door and tried the brass doorknob, but it would not open. Looking up she saw an opening about fifty feet above where she stood. She climbed up the stones on the side of the fortress until she was inside the opening.

The inside was even creepier than the outside. A steady stream of insects skittered across the damp floor, like a living carpet. The walls had the same moss as the outside; the smell of brimstone filed the air.

Sandra slowly walked into the main part of the fortress, suddenly the wizard appeared. He stood more than six feet tall, his long white bread hung down from his wrinkled face. His deep blue robe and hat was covered with silver and gold stars. Sandra ducked inside another doorway and dashed through twisting, curving hallways. The wizard was right on her tail.

She needed a plan to defeat the wizard and save the prince. Just ahead she saw another doorway. Running towards the door she pushed against it. Inside she saw books, tubes and pipes running all across a table. She was inside the wizard's laboratory. She began to search for a map to show her where the prince was being kept.

Suddenly the door opened and the wizard stepped inside, He waved his hand in a wide circle and a hole opened up behind Sandra, and with a blast of blue magic the wizard sent Sandra through the hole.

Sandra tumbled down a dark tunnel with her eyes squeezed firmly shut. Suddenly she stopped moving. When she opened her eyes she was sitting on a stone floor in the dungeon.

A weak voice whispered in the darkness 'Who are you?"

Sandra moved closer to the voice, "I am Sandra. Are you the prince? I am here to help you. I will have you out of here as soon as I can."

Sandra quickly untied the prince and they made their way up a winding staircase. At the top of the stairs was a heavy oak door.

Just then an angry voice came from the other side. I suppose you thought you could rescue the prince. Well, I have other plans for you." With that the wizard sent a blast of magic towards Sandra and sent her flying through the air.

When she landed, she saw the fair and everyone came running. Darlene and Lucy grabbed her asking if she was alright and where had she been they had been looking for her for hours.

"The Prince where is the prince? I must save him!"

Sandra ran back towards the tavern and entered inside. Nothing was as it was before; she looked around for the young boy who was there before.

"Sandra where are you?" a voice whispered 'Please come back."

Sandra turned and looked everywhere for the prince but he was nowhere to be seen. Lucy placed her arm around Sandra and led her to a bench.

A shadow fell across Sandra, and she looked up, into the smiling face of the green knight. He looked just like the prince she had been sent to rescue.

"Are you alright Miss? Please drink this cup of mead. It will refresh you."

Sandra smiled as she looked into his eyes. She knew he was saved, she had found the prince. And knew there really was magic in the world.

The End

www.ingramcontent.com/pod-product-compliance
Lightning Source LLC
Chambersburg PA
CBHW050917120626
46552CB00004B/1629